Courage and Wisdom
The Story of Mulan
The Daughter and the Warrior

By Gang Yi & Xiao Guo
Illustrated by Xunzhi Yin

U.S. Sunny Publishing Inc.

Preface

The story of Mulan is passed on in the form of an ancient Chinese poem. It tells of a girl who joined the army in place of her father. She battled enemies for more than a decade before returning home in victory. Though the brutal battles ended long ago, her beautiful story lives on.

People living on the southern side of the protective Great Wall lived comfortable and peaceful lives. But nomadic tribes from the North, known as the Rouran, were increasing in strength. They often crossed the Great Wall to plunder those in the South. Every person in the South had a duty to fight the invaders, and the war dragged on year after year.

Acknowledgments
We would like to thank Aileen Cho, who helped edit the translated text.

FIRST EDITION
Courage and Wisdom——The Story of Mulan

Published in the United States of America by
U.S. Sunny Publishing Inc.
P.O.Box 1264 Stafford, TX 77497

Translator: John Jianhong Xu & Yanfei Wang
Editor   : Caiming Yan & Jiangnan Yi
Art Editor : Huiqing Wan & Dong Xu

ISBN:978-0-9744840-0-6

Library of Congress Control Number
LCCN:2007921295

http://www.ussunnypublishing.com

Printed in China

Mulan was a pretty girl who lived in a small village in China. Her mother taught her how to sew and embroider, while her father taught her archery and horseback riding.

Mulan's father had been a brave soldier, but over time he gradually grew old and weak. Her mother did all the housework. Mulan had an older sister and a younger brother. Everyone in the family worked hard and lived happily together.

When Mulan was 15 years old, the Rouran began to invade the southern lands. The invasion threatened the lives of the local people.

The Rouran tribes lived in the desert and grassland regions, where food was scarce. They envied the wealth and luxury of the southerners, and so they treated the southerners violently. They plundered their goods and killed people who resisted them. Not even the women or children were spared.

The situation had worsened. Smoke from signal towers along the Great Wall warned the southern army of the Rouran's new invasion. One day, the Rouran tribes launched a major invasion and broke through the border defenses. The emperor's messenger rode as fast as possible to spread the word. People in the border towns had to flee.

The government responded quickly to the emergency and called on all men to join the army. By law, every adult man had to serve. Mulan's father also was drafted, even though he was ill and weak. That night, Mulan worried that her father might be too weak to survive the war. And her younger brother was only eight years old. "Now only I can help my father," Mulan contemplated.

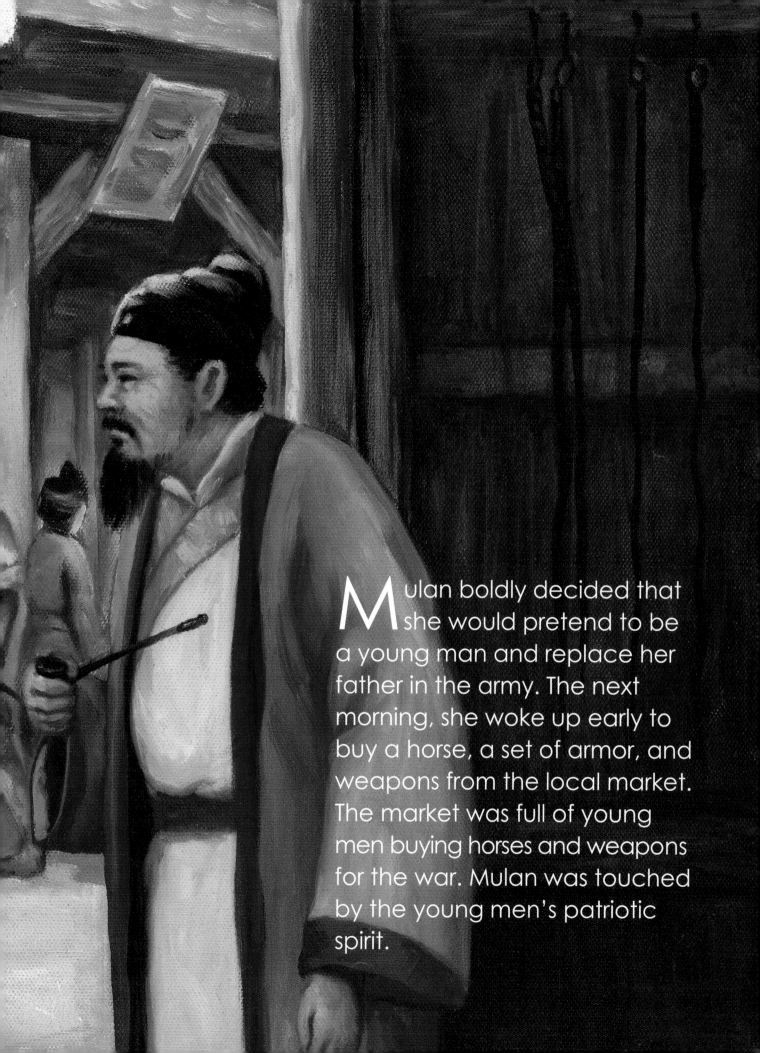

Mulan boldly decided that she would pretend to be a young man and replace her father in the army. The next morning, she woke up early to buy a horse, a set of armor, and weapons from the local market. The market was full of young men buying horses and weapons for the war. Mulan was touched by the young men's patriotic spirit.

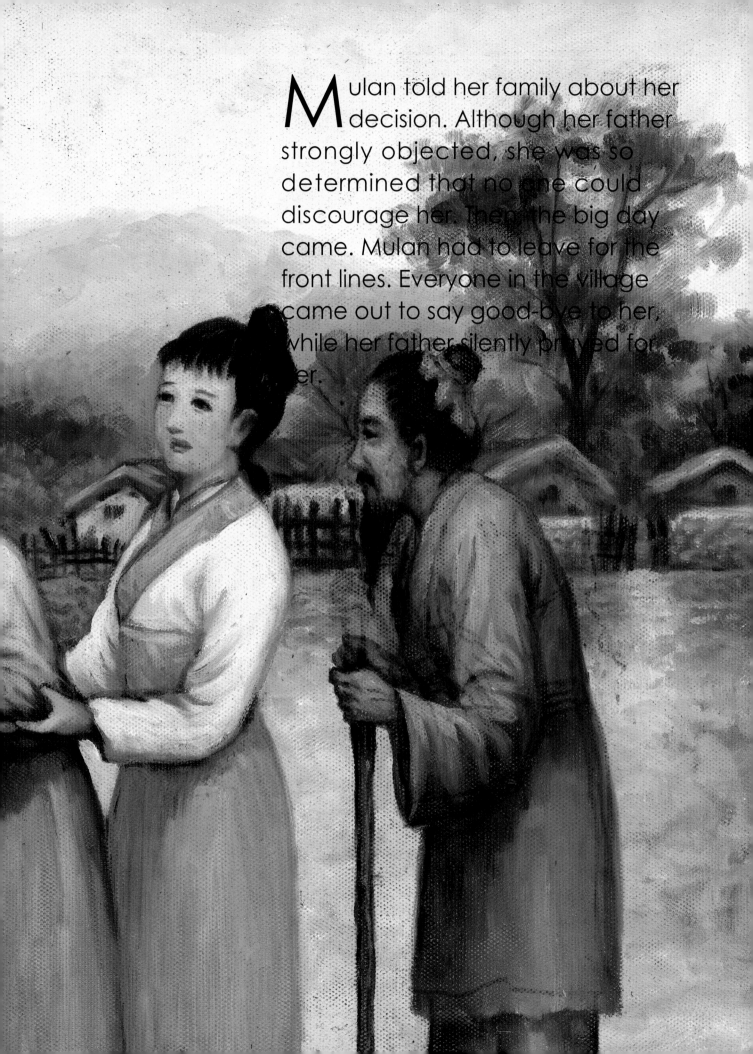

Mulan told her family about her decision. Although her father strongly objected, she was so determined that no one could discourage her. Then the big day came. Mulan had to leave for the front lines. Everyone in the village came out to say good-bye to her, while her father silently prayed for her.

Mulan, disguised as a young man, rode toward the front lines. Everywhere, passionate young men were heading in the same direction. Together, they rode past mountains and rivers, moving ever closer to the front. From a distance came the neighing of horses. The young soldiers were motivated and ready to fight.

Soldiers from all regions arrived at the campsite, ready for the commanders to assign them positions and duties. They all were geared up to fight the enemy with every ounce of energy in their bodies. Like the others, Mulan was determined to do her best.

Mulan began the tough pre-battle training. She did not mind pain and showed no sign of weakness. Her skills in fighting improved rapidly and rivaled those of the young men. No one suspected that she was a girl.

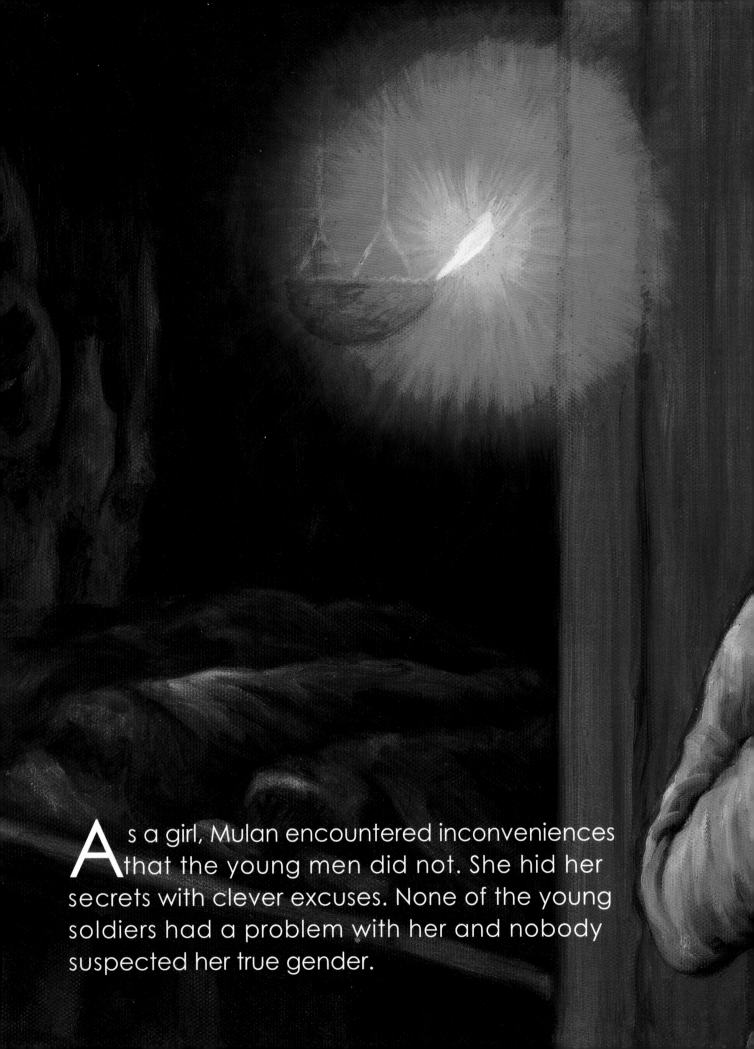

As a girl, Mulan encountered inconveniences that the young men did not. She hid her secrets with clever excuses. None of the young soldiers had a problem with her and nobody suspected her true gender.

Mulan fought bravely. Although she was small, she always fought at the forefront. Soon, she won praise from her commanders and comrades. They frequently defeated the nomadic tribes.

The war against the nomadic tribes continued endlessly, like a tug-of-war. Every time the enemies lost, they would return to counterattack. Gradually, as she got older, Mulan grew more mature, as well as becoming an ever better soldier. Whenever there was a break in the fighting, she could not help thinking of home. She often dreamed about her parents and siblings.

Mulan's excellent performance won her numerous awards, and eventually she was promoted to assistant commander. She helped to plan the battle strategy, frequently coming up with ingenious ideas to defeat the enemy.

One day, Mulan sneaked into the enemy's camp with a small team to confront them. The tribal leader awoke and led his main army in a fight against Mulan and her soldiers. Mulan and her soldiers fled and, in their rush, left behind countless weapons.

The tribal leader thought that Mulan and her small team were running for their lives, so he led his men and chased them. He wanted to capture Mulan alive. Mulan and her men hurried through a valley between two towering mountains.

The tribal leader and his men chased Mulan and her team into the valley, but they found no one. Yet, they kept on chasing. When the whole tribal army arrived in the valley, a sudden burst of drums sounded; stones rolled down from hilltops and arrows flew across the sky. The tribal army, terrified, fell into chaos and soon lost morale.

The tribal leader tried to escape with his guards, but Mulan and her soldiers blocked their way. They had been leading the enemy into a trap all along. Finally, they caught the tribal leader. After twelve years of war, the enemy's main army surrendered.

After twelve years of war, the enemy had been defeated, its leader helpless in captivity. This marked a magnificent victory for Mulan's country. Everyone was happy because the long war had finally ended, and they could return to their normal lives. As the news spread, everyone came out to celebrate in the streets. The ministers and the people stood along the streets to welcome the victorious army, which was escorting the captured tribal leader back to the capital.

Mulan had played a huge part in her country's victory. The emperor, pleased with her achievements, awarded her an abundance of gold, silver, and jewelry. He also invited her to serve in the army ministry. Mulan knelt down and replied to the emperor, "Thank you very much, your Majesty! It is my duty to serve my country. I do not deserve these awards. Now that the world is peaceful once again, my only wish is to return home and care for my aging parents. I beg you to allow me to return home!"

The emperor continued to try to persuade Mulan to stay, but she was so determined to go home that he had no choice but to let her go. Mulan bade farewell to her comrades at the long pavilion. After twelve years together in the battlefields, they had become lifelong friends, even though they still did not know that she was a woman. It was painful to say good-bye to each other. They agreed to visit her some day. After her farewell, Mulan could not wait to rush home to meet her family.

After twelve years, Mulan's parents had grown much older. With bent backs and teary eyes, they came out to meet her. Her younger brother had grown up and was grinding his knife to chop meat when she arrived. Her sister was busy cleaning Mulan's room and putting up decorations. Everyone was so happy to have her back, and she was happy to finally be home. The whole family lived a peaceful life forever after.

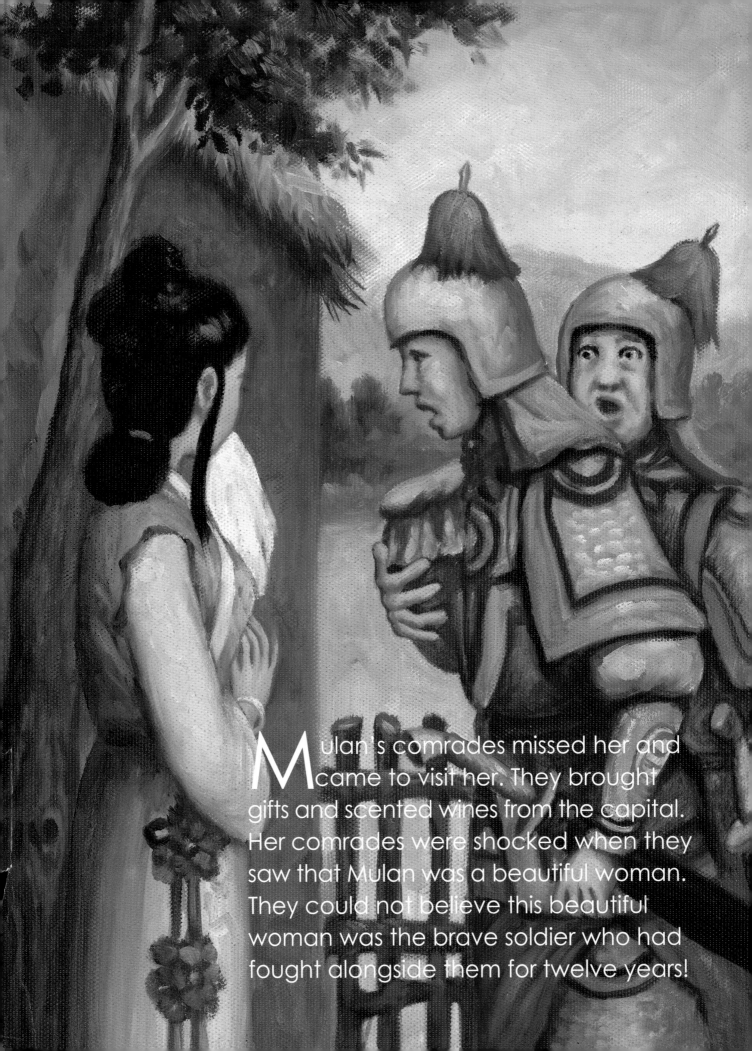

Mulan's comrades missed her and came to visit her. They brought gifts and scented wines from the capital. Her comrades were shocked when they saw that Mulan was a beautiful woman. They could not believe this beautiful woman was the brave soldier who had fought alongside them for twelve years!